I0669640

John Shebbeare

A Letter to the People of England

on the necessity of putting an immediate end to the war - and the means

of obtaining an advantageous peace

John Shebbeare

A Letter to the People of England
on the necessity of putting an immediate end to the war - and the means of obtaining an advantageous peace

ISBN/EAN: 9783337224721

Printed in Europe, USA, Canada, Australia, Japan

Cover: Foto ©Andreas Hilbeck / pixelio.de

More available books at **www.hansebooks.com**

A

LETTER

TO THE

PEOPLE of ENGLAND,

ON THE

NECESSITY of putting an Immediate
End to the WAR;

AND

The MEANS of obtaining an Advantageous
PEACE.

Premenda occasio.——

LONDON:

Printed for R. GRIFFITHS, opposite Somerset-
House, in the Strand. MDCCLX.

Countrymen and Friends,

IT is inconceivable, to Slaves of other Nations, in what Degree every Individual in this Kingdom may juſtly boaſt himſelf to have a Share, as well in giving Laws to his Country, as in the immediate Adminiſtration of its Government.

The Sovereign, indeed, makes Choice of his Miniſters, and the People have their Repreſentatives in Parliament; but neither, by the Allegiance they pay the one, nor the Confidence they place in the other, do *Britons* give up this natural Right, to be ſtill Maſters of their own Properties, and Guardians of their own Liberties.

The recent Experience of a few Years paſt may furniſh us with ſtriking Inſtances, how loud the Voice of the People is heard in *England*, both on the Throne and in the Senate; Inſtances, that prove the vaſt Importance of its being diſtinguiſhed from the impetuous Clamour of a factious Multitude, by its Conformity to the more ſober Dictates of Reaſon and Truth. *Non omninò temerè fit, quod vulgò dictitant.*

It is to you, therefore, my Fellow-Countrymen, and not to any of thoſe great men, whoſe Importance depends, in ſo eminent a Degree, on the Conformity of their Conduct to the Voice of the Public, that I conceive it neceſſary to addreſs myſelf at this Juncture.

B   Amidſt

Amidst the Preparations for acting fresh Scenes of Slaughter and Desolation, the ensuing Campaign, a *Peace* is sometimes talked of; and we are flattered by many that it is near at Hand. God grant it may! A favourable Prospect, indeed, presents itself, of obtaining a no less honourable than lasting one, if we trifle not with the present Opportunity, and the enemy be, as it is surmised, really desirous of putting an immediate end to the War.

But, perhaps, the latter is not so certain as is commonly imagined; and, with respect to the former, I confess it, I am not without my Fears. For I will make no Scruple to declare it of the utmost Consequence to this Nation, that the expected Treaty should be hastened, by all the prudent Means the most artful Negotiator can suggest; and that for us wilfully to run the Hazard of unnecessary Delays, will be as impolitic, as the Consequences may be dangerous.

In our present Circumstances, it might ill become us to sue for Peace; but, to offer reasonable Terms of Accommodation, and to enter readily into every Measure, consistent with our Honour and Interest, to facilitate it, may, I presume, be, without Difficulty, proved not only expedient but necessary.

You have, indeed, been frequently told, on this Occasion, that you are under no Necessity to have recourse to the Arts of Negotiation; that you are in a Condition to impose your own

Terms

Terms on the vanquifhed Enemy; and that, in your Circumftances as Victors, you fhould deliberate at Leifure on a Peace; for no Delay can be dangerous. But have thefe nota le Advifers affured you how long we fhall remain in thefe victorious Circumftances? Have they monopolized the Means of Succefs, and left nothing to the future Fortune of War? You may remember we were not always Victors; and it would not be improper to reflect, we may not always continue fuch.

As it is not my Defign, however, to indulge romantic Hopes and ill grounded Expectations on the one Hand; fo, on the other, I do not mean to encourage chimerical Sufpicions, or intimidate with groundlefs Fears. I cannot conceive, neverthelefs, that we have any fufficient Reafon to prefume the Hand of Providence will always continue to be exerted in fo wonderful a Manner, as it has lately been, in our Favour. As Prefcience is not the Gift of Humanity, it is therefore, by the general Experience of paft Times, and the common Courfe of Events, that we muft regulate our Conduct.

On the prefent Occafion then, let us calmly confider what has contributed to thofe Events, that have fo furprifingly elated this Nation, and depreffed its Enemies. Let us take an impartial View of our different Circumftances at prefent, and thence judge by Probability of the future.

B 2

Perhaps,

Perhaps, notwithſtanding all the Reaſon we have had, of late, to be ſatisfied with the Meaſures of a wiſe and prudent Adminiſtration ; notwithſtanding all the juſt Encomiums ſo freely made on the Conduct of our Commanders, and the Intrepidity of our Troops ; if Partiality to ourſelves were entirely laid aſide, we ſhould find our late Succeſs no leſs owing to a providential Concurrence of fortunate Circumſtances, than either to miniſterial Wiſdom or military Valour.

In like Manner, were our real Situation duly attended to, notwithſtanding the Advantages we have gained of the Enemy, we ſhould, perhaps, find little Reaſon for our immoderate Triumph. Perhaps alſo, thoſe Advantages would be found leſs deciſive, and the Enemies Loſſes leſs irreparable, or at leaſt much leſs ruinous and intolerable, than we now are apt to flatter ourſelves they are.

Reſpecting the Means of our Succeſs; it would be an invidious Taſk to enter minutely into Particulars, and might be conſtrued into a malevolent Deſign of depreciating the Merit of many, to whoſe gallant or prudent Behaviour, in their reſpective Stations, their Country is ſo greatly indebted.

But, without diſparaging the Conduct of any of thoſe, who may have deſerved well at the Hands of their Fellow-Countrymen, without caſting the leaſt Soil, by Reflection, on the Luſtre of their Characters, it may be juſtly aſſerted ferted that fome of our late Expeditions have been ill planned, and worfe directed; and that the Defign of others, as well as the Perfons and Means employed to carry them into Execution, have been ill adapted to fuch arduous Enterprizes. This has been palpable enough, where we have been unfuccefsful; as the feveral Blunders made on the Coaft of *France*, and in *North America*, may inglorioufly teftify. And if, in fome others more prudently directed, we have been fo happy as to fucceed, has it not rather been owing to adventitious Circumftances, and the greateft good Fortune in the World, than to the Meafures calculated to infure Succefs?

I will not infift on our fhameful Mifcarriage at *Rochfort*, or foolifh Retreat at *St. Cas*; the Siege of *Quebec*, and the Battle of *Minden* are our favourite Objects of Triumph. But if our Expedition againft the former had not fucceeded, (and how great a Chance has it appeared that it did not!) might it not, at this Time, have been reprefented as a wrong-headed Enterprize, favouring of Quixotifm, and tending only to the Deftruction of the Adventurers; who were too few, too ill fupplied, or too ill directed, to carry their Point? Might not the projected Affiftance of our *American* Troops, in the Neighbourhood of *Crown-Point*, have been virulently exploded, as (it indeed appears to have been) premature and chimerical? Might it not have been efteemed a grofs Inftance of

Ignorance

Ignorance or Imprudence in the Projectors of such an Armament, to have made the most formidable Part of it such, as the very Nature of the Place would render useless; while, at the same Time, they had sent only a handful of brave Men to oppose the whole Force of *Canada* *? Nay, might not hence the whole Design have been condemned, as a futile and insufficient Attempt, unadvisedly and foolishly calculated to sacrifice our Men and Money, without effectually indemnifying ourselves, or annoying the Enemy?

This might have been done; I may venture to assert, it would have been done, and would have obtained Credit too, among Thousands of those who now attribute to the Wisdom of the Administration, and the Greatness of our military Force, that Success, which the late brave Man, to whom we owe it, once despaired of, and, urged perhaps by that Motive, to a most desperate Attempt, was himself the only Means of obtaining, at the Expence of his Life, I say only Means, as it is more than probable, in the Circumstances the Besiegers then were, that no

---

* By the Nature of the River, the most formidable Part of this Armament is deprived of the Power of acting, yet we have almost the whole Force of *Canada* to oppose.—The Affairs of *Great Britain*, I know, require vigorous Measures; but then the Courage of a Handful of brave Men should be exerted only where there is some Hope of a favourable Event.
Wolfe's Letter to Secretary PITT.

other

other General in the Service (without the leaſt
Diſparagement to the Bravery of any) would
have hazarded the Attempt, which crowned
their Enterprize with Succeſs. Nay, perhaps,
had it not been attended with that Succeſs, the
Attempt itſelf might have been condemned, by
Men more cautious than bold, as raſh and
imprudent.

Again, the Battle of *Minden* was as unpro-
vided for as the Victory was unexpected; nay,
certain it is, that the Commander in chief was
ſo powerfully poſſeſſed of the Notion that he
muſt be defeated, if he ſhould be forced, at
that Time, into a Battle, that he could hardly
credit the Fact, when, by an amazing Inſtance
of Valour in the *Britiſh* Infantry, he ſaw the
Enemy beaten out of the Field.

Is it now from the miraculous Succeſs of un-
timely and ill-planned Projects; is it from the
accidental Gain of deſperate Battles, into which
we have been ſurprized, and wherein Victory
turned only on the ſuperior Bravery of a Handful of Men, that we confidently promiſe ourſelves Security and future Conqueſt? It may be
remembered, the Plains of *Fontenoy*, as well as
thoſe of *Minden*, have witneſſed the Superiority
of *Britiſh* Valour, though not with equal Succeſs.

Nunc pluit, et claro nunc Jupiter æthre fulget.

But,

But, leaving this apparently invidious Subject, let us confider what Reafons we may have
to flatter ourfelves with the Continuation of our
prefent Superiority in the War, either from our
own peculiar Abilities to profecute it, or thofe
which our late Advantages over the Enemy may
have given us.

Perhaps, a View of our prefent Circumftances,
ftript of that Glofs and falfe Colouring, which
recent Succefs has thrown upon the Perfpeɛtive,
will not be pleafing. Nay, were it not contrafted
to fome Advantage by the more cloudy Profpeɛt
of the Situation of the Enemy, it were enough
to make us tremble at our own.

The Government an hundred Millions in
Debt, the neceffary Expences of the War in-
creafing this immenfe Sum yearly, by additional
Millions, in what can this monftrous Burthen of
national Credit end? Will not the enormous
Weight of fuch a Debt very foon infallibly crufh
the Author of its Being? Nay, what fhall we
not have to fear on this Account, even though a
fpeedy Peace fhould enable us to fit down with
only a few Millions added to the prefent Sum?

Might we not, in fpeaking on this Subjeɛt,
join heartily with the zealous Patriot, who lately
expreffed his Apprehenfions for the Independency
of the Conftitution, when refleɛting on that infinite Dependance on the Crown, that has been
created by Means of the national *Debt* * ?

* See a Letter to *Two Great Men,* p. 44.

Does

Does not another Confideration, alfo, as little attended to as greatly important, naturally arife, when we think on the Numbers of thofe who are fupported in Indolence or Luxury, by the Intereft of the Funds? Indolence in every State is deftructive; and though moderate Luxury (if fuch an Expreffion may be ufed) in Poffeffors and Cultivators of Land, in Artifts, Manufacturers, &c. may have its Ufe, as it can be fupported only by Ingenuity and Induftry, in the Cultivation of the mechanical or economical Arts; yet nothing can be more pernicious than the Luxury of thofe, who live idly on the Labour of others.

There are Men, it is true, fo fhort-fighted as to fuppofe the Confumption of thofe Commodities, from which the Government draws its Revenues, fo neceffary, that, while the Proprietors of Stock fpend their Income at home, they conceive them to act the Part of ufeful Citizens, and to be profitable Members to the Commonwealth. Did Art or Nature, indeed, fo generoufly reward the Labour of Individuals, by fo plentifully providing them thereby, with the Articles of Convenience or Luxury, as to afford befides a Superfluity of thofe Articles for others, thefe ufelefs *Confumers* might be overlooked as infignificant: But, fince the Cafe is far otherwife, it is evident the whole Tribe of Stock-holding Gentry, with their numerous Attendants, are fupported at the Expence of the

C   landed

landed and laborious Part of the Nation; and, though made Ufe of as the Means of raifing the Taxes, inftead of facilitating their Payment, add grievoufly to the Burthen and increafe the Difficulty of fupporting it.

As the Increafe of Taxes, alfo, tends to increafe the Number of Stock-holders, fo muft the Price of all the Means of Life, and confequently of Labour, increafe, till it come to a Degree incompatible with the Profperity, or even the Being, of many of our Manufactories.

It is further a melancholy Reflection to think, in how many Inftances the Neceffity of raifing fuch vaft Sums as the Exigencies of State require, contributes to promote Idlenefs and Debauchery, in the lower Claffes of People. It may be fufficient here to hint only at the Diftillery; and barely to mention the Cafe of Tipling Houfes, the unlimited Number of which are fo pernicious to the Morals and Manners of thofe, on whom both the Wealth and Strength of the Nation ultimately depend.

Can it be denied that in thefe, as in many other Cafes, the moft prudential Maxims of domeftick Polity have not been difpenfed with, under Pretence of the Neceffity of promoting the Revenue? Nothing, indeed, can be more abfurd than to imagine the Duties, arifing from the Means of Intoxication, Debilitation and Riot, more beneficial to a ftate, than Sobriety

and

and Regularity of Manners: but while Thoufands find their Intereft fo intimately connected with the increafe of the Revenues, it is no wonder, while fuch a Plea is at Hand, that it fhould be too often made Ufe of, to dangerous Purpofes.

Waving thefe Confiderations, however, as perhaps too general for the prefent Occafion, let me afk, if the Weight of this Incumbrance is not likely very foon to affect us too fenfibly, in the Means of carrying on the War? Can it be conceived that the Danger attending our immenfe Debt is ftill at too great a Diftance to be feared, or provided againft? May we not be faid to have already felt the contrary? Reflect on the mortifying Inftance of the Lofs the Sub-fcribers fuftained laft Year, in being obliged, many of them, to fell out, at almoft Twenty per Cent. under *Par*. Tell me at what Price does their Stock ftand now?

The World may, for awhile, be blinded by the fecret Allowance of Premiums to large Subfcribers; but this Method of raifing Money, if ever it fhould be practifed, cannot laft long. I know Occafion has been taken, from our hav-ing been able to provide fo *immenfely* for the Supplies of another Year, to boaft that the like may be done for Years to come *. If it be put to the Proof, we fhall, perhaps, find

* See Letter to Two Great Men, p. 51.

C 2

our-

ourfelves greatly miftaken. I hope, therefore, we fhall not run the Rifque of fo mortifying a Difappointment; which, after our inordinate boafting, may fubject us to the Ridicule of all Europe.

But, fuppofing we may yet borrow, at the Hazard of National Ruin, five or fix Millions annually, for fome Time longer; at what rate is this Money to be had? It is moft infallibly certain that we muft foon give greater Intereft than we have as yet done; and perhaps than the Purpofes for which we borrow will enable us to pay.

The Rife of Intereft was plainly forefeen laft Year; and, though the critical Bankruptcy of the French Government gave ours a temporary Advantage in their late Subfcription, do we not fee the Adventurers already in a fair Way of repenting their Bargain?

Reflect on the ordinary Expences of Government, at the prefent Juncture. From twelve to fourteen Millions Sterling annually! What an immenfe Sum! It may have been neceffary. It may have been well applied. But, for God's fake, what poffible Advantages can we think to gain, by continuing the War beyond the prefent Period, fufficient to indemnify us even in the Article only of thefe exorbitant Expences?

In anfwer to this Queftion, we are naturally led to the more pleafing Profpect of our Circum-ftances, relieved by Contraft with thofe of the Enemy.

Enemy. On a careful Infpection, however, favourable as it is, even this may be found to afford us too barren a View, to give us hope of reaping a more glorious Harveft by the Profecution of the War.

As I have not exaggerated our own Situation, refpecting the Rifque our National Credit will infallibly run, by continuing the War, and our Inabilities to carry it on, but at the Hazard of domeftick Ruin; I fhall admit only of as juft a Reprefentation of the Circumftances of the Enemy. I fhall not fcruple to fay, therefore, thefe have been much exaggerated; as future Experience will, in all Probability, convince you.

That the French Nation have fuffered extremely in their Navigation and Commerce, and confequently the State muft be greatly diftreffed in its Finances, are undoubted Truths; fuch, indeed, as we cannot reflect upon, as Britons, but with the greateft Satisfaction. Stript of their Colonies, and ruined in their Marine, they are undoubtedly, as a commercial and maritime Nation, reduced low indeed. But let us not plume ourfelves too much on this Reflection. France is ftill formidable as a military Power; ftill capable of doing an infinite deal of Mifchief to others, though but little of benefiting itfelf.

However exhaufted its Finances; however ruined in its Trade; it hath ftill its Refources.

It

It is a Country to which Nature has been fo indulgent, that it is not eafily eat up at home; and what is it that a Sovereign, who is in a great Degree abfolute Mafter of the Lives and Pro-perties of his Subjects, cannot effect, when urged by the Neceffities of the Times to take defperate Meafures to fupport a defperate Caufe.

God grant, indeed, their Caufe be actually fo ruinous as the leaft fanguine among us fuppofe. And yet, perhaps, Circumftances, really def-perate, may, eventually at leaft, be the worft a Nation, prudently defirous of a Peace, fhould wifh their Enemy reduced to. To have little or nothing more to lofe that can be loft; and to have every Thing to hope, that can at all be hoped for, from their Perfeverance in the War, are not Motives to excite them to fpeedy Terms of Accommodation.

On the contrary, will not fuch Motives na-turally induce them to try the Fortune of ano-ther, and yet another, Campaign? at the End of which, who can tell how far our own Situa-tion may be comparatively changed for the worfe? *Nefcis quid ferus vefper vebit.*

It has, indeed, been roundly afferted, and that with the moft egregious Affurance, that 'it is entirely owing to the *German* Part of the 'prefent War, that France *appears* fo low in the political Scale of Strength and Riches,

'that

' that she is *found to be* a sinking Monarchy, nay
' a Monarchy already sunk.'

' Full of the Project,' it is said, ' of con-
' quering *Hanover*, she saw herself obliged to en-
' gage in exorbitant Expences; Armies were to
' be paid and maintained in Westphalia, and
' on the Rhine; vast Sums were to be ad-
' vanced to the Court of *Vienna*, always as in-
' digent as it is haughty; the ravenous Ruf-
' fians, and the degenerate Swedes, would not
' move unless allured by Subsidies; and the
' Mouth of every hungry *German* Prince was to
' be stopt with the *Louis d'ors* of *France*. In-
' volved in Expences thus enormous, our Ene-
' mies have been prevented from strengthening
' themselves at Sea, where England had most
' Reason to dread their becoming strong *.'

This declamatory Method of Argumentation,
however plausible it may seem, is little con-
clusive. General Assertions prove nothing. It
is not, for Instance, made as yet very clear that
the Conquest of *Hanover* cost *France* such an
immense Sum in the Acquisition, as is here
hinted at.

The Armies maintained in Westphalia, and
on the Rhine, cost the French Government
little more (I have been told less) than they
would have done, had those Troops been all
the while idling at home. And, in general, the

* Letter to Two Great Men, p. 36, 37, 38.

great

great Number of Men which the French keep
on foot, even in Time of Peace, makes the additional Expence of a War on the Continent
much lefs to them than is commonly imagined
by us, on whom the Maintenance of a handful
falls fo burthenfome. In fact, alfo, the Quan-
tum of the Subfidies paid by the Enemy to their
Allies, during this War, has not been fo pro-
digious as to impoverifh them fo much as you
have been taught to believe. No; it has not
been the *continental* but the *naval* Part of the
War, in which the natural Force of Great Britain has been properly exerted, that has reduced
France fo low in the political Scale of Strength
and Riches.

That the Enemy's Want of Money, occafioned by the exorbitant Expence of their Alliances
and the Maintenance of their Armies in Germany, was the only, or at leaft the principal
Reafon, that prevented their ftrengthening themfelves by Sea, is a Pofition, indeed, almoft too
abfurd to be debated. There is not a Man of
Common Senfe in the Kingdom, but muft be
fenfible that the Lofs they fuftained, before and
after the formal Declaration of War, by the
Capture of their Ships, and the Detention of
their Seamen in our Prifons, was more effectual
in preventing their ftrengthening themfelves by
Sea than all the extraordinary Engagements they
have entered into, or Armies they have paid and
fupported on the Continent.

After

After the War broke out, alfo, many Difficulties prefented themfelves, from their Want
of Materials for building, repairing and equip-
ping their Ships, which no Money, had they
ever fo much in the Treafury, or were their Finances in ever fuch good order, could ob-
viate.

With refpect to Hanover too, it is certain
that, had they been as fuccefsful in keeping, as
in acquiring it, they would have found themfelves Gainers by the Expedition; abftracted
from the Confideration of what general Ufe it
might have been to them, in profecuting the
War, or in negotiating a Peace. It is notorious
that Hanover fell an eafy Sacrifice: And there
is Reafon to believe that, had not that expe-
rienced and able General *, who conquered it,
been obliged to leave the Army, on Account of
the Intrigues and Cabals of his perfonal Enemies at Court, his great Prudence and Fore-
fight would have taken fuch Meafures as would
have more effectually fecured its Poffeffion:
Even as it was, however, the accidental Mortality
among their Troops undoubtedly operated more
than any other Caufe to the Enemy's evacuating
that Electorate.

It is not without fufficient Reafon, alfo,
fhould it be afferted that the Caufe why they
have not been already in Poffeffion of it again,
is rather owing to the clafhing of perfonal Interefts at Court, and divided Councils both in the

* Marfhal D'Etrées.

D   Cabi-

Cabinet and the Field, than to their natural In-
ability, either from want of Men or Money, to
profecute the War on the Side of Germany with
Succefs.

This having been the Cafe, who can tell but
repeated Ill-Succefs may have the fame Effect on
the disjointed Councils of France as it had, not
long fince, on thofe of this Kingdom? Self-
intereft and private Refentment may fubfide; Mi-
nifters and Commanders may unite to do their
Duty; and the Confequence, as in our own Cafe,
be the Revival of a difpirited, defpifed People
to Conqueft and to Glory.

Confider, my Fellow Countrymen, what a
mortifying Stroke this will prove to us, after
having indulged ourfelves, as we now do, in the
utmoft Excefs of Triumph and Exultation. Let
us not, therefore, give Occafion for it by relying
too much on the Diftrefs and fuppofed Weaknefs of the Enemy.

This, at leaft, is certain; that they may reap
fome Advantages, as to their future Abilities of
carrying on the War, even from their ill Fortune. The Gain flowing into the Treafury, from
the Duties laid on the Articles of their extenfive
Commerce, is, indeed, put a Stop to. But, at
the fame Time, on the other hand, the Charge of
fupporting a large Marine, and a diftant expenfive Colony, is rendered needlefs, by the Deftruction of the one and the Lofs of the other. They
will, therefore, hardly, for the future, fit out
Fleets at a great Expence to fail without an Er-
rand,

rand, or freight Ships only to be taken. Fatal Experience will, doubtless, teach them a Leſſon we ourſelves have ſo greatly profited by, notwithſtanding we appear at preſent ſo very willing to unlearn it again; which is, to employ their natural Strength againſt their Enemies, and puſh with all their Force on that Element and in that Quarter, where their Endeavours are moſt likely to ſucceed.

They ſee, or have Reaſon enough to ſee, very plainly, that their Trade and Colonies are indefenſible by any Effort they can now make with their Marine; and that it may be as well to let their few remaining Ships of War rot in their Harbours, as to fit them out only to fall into the Hands of the Enemy. They have, therefore, no other probable Way of indemnifying themſelves for the Loſſes already ſuſtained, or of prevailing on us to accede to a Treaty of Peace on any Terms, ſhort of the moſt diſgraceful and diſadvantageous, than to proſecute the War with all their Force in Germany.

To do this, they will probably begin to think of aſſiſting the Queen of Hungary in earneſt, and puſh forward to make themſelves again Maſters of Hanover: In which Caſe, who can pretend to ſay what may be our Situation at the End of another Campaign?

You have been told that we ſhall, in all Probability, loſe none of the Advantages gained in the laſt Campaign, by the enſuing one, ' if our ' Army, ſtill headed by Prince *Ferdinand*, who

has

' has already gained fo many Laurels, be render-
' ed more formidable by fending to it *fome Thou-*
' *fands* more of our national Troops *.' I hope
we fhall not; but as to the Probability of it, I
muft confefs I am of another Opinion. Not that
I doubt the Capacity of Prince Ferdinand, the
Conduct of our prefent Britifh Generals, or the
Valour of our Troops. But unlefs, inftead of
fome Thoufands, we could fend *as many* as we
fhould have Reafon to think would fuffice, I
conceive it more probable that we fhall lofe, than
gain, Advantages in that Quarter.

I have already mentioned that our Succefs in the
laft Campaign was in a great Degree accidental,
and very reafonably unexpected; nor can I be
perfuaded that we fhall, or indeed that we have it
in our Power, to augment Prince Ferdinand's
Army fo much as the French can, and actually
will, do theirs.

We may flatter ourfelves that they will be prevented from fending fufficient Supplies into Germany, left we fhould again make Attempts on
their Coafts. But what fufficient Reafon have we
to think this will be really the Cafe? Let thofe,
who pretend that the prefent diftreffed Condition
of France is *entirely* owing to the German Part
of the War, tell us, whether her Coafts were left
unguarded when her Troops laft invaded Hanover. Did we find her Coafts, in fact, fo defti-
tute of Troops when we were lately facrificing
our Men and Money in expenfive Expeditions,
that neither paid Cofts, or did us Honour? It is

* Letter to Two Great Men.

true,

true, we deſtroyed one of the Enemy's Ports, and levied Contributions on a few petty Villages; which done, they had nothing more to fear, nor did they on that Occaſion recal one ſingle Regiment from Germany.

You may ſtill ſay, indeed, that though they were not obliged on any particular Occaſion to recall their Forces, the Apprehenſion of the Conſequences of thoſe Expeditions in general, prevented them primarily from ſending more. This, however, is to aſſert a Negative that cannot eaſily be proved.

But, be this as it will, certain it is, they did not appear on thoſe Occaſions under any great Apprehenſions for the Event of ſuch Attempts; well knowing in what they muſt neceſſarily end. And can it be ſuppoſed they will be much more ſo now, when even the Security of their Ports is of leſs Conſequence to them, than at the Beginning of the War? as in their preſent Situation they cannot hope to recruit their Marine, ſo far during the War as to cope with us again at Sea.

Can this be ſuppoſed, I ſay, when they muſt be effectually convinced that their acting merely on the defenſive can be to no Purpoſe? Let us ſuppoſe them then ever ſo hard put to it to find Troops to guard their Coaſts, and at the ſame Time to puſh the German War, we have all the Reaſon in the World to think they will exert every Limb, ſtrain every Nerve, and at leaſt neglect nothing to inſure Succeſs on the Side of Germany, where only perhaps any Thing can now be done

to

to retrieve their shattered Affairs. Instead, therefore, of the Probability being on the Side of those
who conceive, we are not likely to lose in another
Campaign the Advantages we gained in the last,
the contrary appears not only probable, but not
unreasonably to be feared, and, indeed, too justly
to be expected.

Consider further the Situation of our brave and
indefatigable Ally, the King of Prussia; who,
after having surprized the admiring World with
the most astonishing Instances of Fortitude and
military Skill, finds himself at length surround-
ed by his Enemies, overpowered by superior
Numbers, his Country exhausted, and his Cause
supported only by those who are in no Situation
to recruit his Armies, and but very little able to
second his Operations.

You may plume yourselves, from the uncom-
mon Difficulties this great Prince hath hitherto
encountered and surmounted, with hopes, that he
will be still able to defend himself from his Enemies, and keep them at bay till they shall be willing
to enter into a Peace, on Terms neither dishonour-
able to himself, or disadvantageous to his Allies.

Be not too sanguine; you may be deceived.
The court of Vienna, indigent as it is, hath powerful Resources. The Empress Queen can never
want Men; and while her Arms are crowned with
any Share of Success, Money, at some rate or
other, will certainly be had.

If we reflect, also, on the present System of
Austrian Policy, adopted by her Neighbours and
Al-

Allies, it is become neceffary to their common Intereft and Security, that the Wings of the towering Eagle of Brandenburg fhould be clipp'd.

Can it be imagined then they will not purfue thofe Advantages, which the prefent embarraffed Situation of his Pruffian Majefty gives them, to accomplifh their Defign : A Defign long premeditated, and which has unhappily been too earneftly purfued.

Should Hanover then again fall a Prey to a rapacious Enemy, or fhould the King of Pruffia be reduced to Extremities, fhould not we be called upon, to deliver the one and extricate the other, by all the Ties of Honour, Juftice and Humanity ? And, can it be thought that, in the Cafe of either, we fhould be able to obtain the fame advantageous Terms of Peace that we might probably do at prefent ?

But we will fuppofe this heroick Prince fhould be able, for fome Time, to fuftain the united Efforts of his Enemies againft him ; that, under the Protection of that Providence, which has hitherto fo fignally interpofed in his Favour, he may continue to detect their Intrigues, to difappoint their Machinations, and ftill to fhare in the Honours and Advantages of the Field. More cannot reafonably be expected. It cannot be expected that, harraffed as he has been, and is, on every Side, in his Perfon, his narrow Diftricts depopulated, his Veterans wafted by continual Slaughter, he fhould be ever, during this War, in a State to reduce his imperious Enemies fo low, as to beg or accept of Peace on his own Terms.

Such

Such an Expectation would be in the higheſt Degree extravagant. The moſt ſanguine of his Friends, the moſt zealous Admirers of his great Qualities, cannot hope this with any ſhew of Reaſon.

Let us ſuppoſe further that, by the Unanimity and prudential Conduct of our Generals, aſſiſted by the Valour of our Troops, the French may be kept out of Hanover. What can we gain at beſt by prolonging the War? How long may we not *ſiege and battle* it on the Continent before we oblige them to accept of Terms more advantageous to this Nation than they may be diſpoſed to do at preſent?

In the mean Time, let me aſk, at whoſe Expence is the King of Pruſſia to be ſupported? At whoſe Coſt is Hanover and the reſt of his Majeſty's German Dominions, and thoſe of his other Allies, to be protected? At whoſe, but at this Nation's? What a Reflection! What waſte of Blood and Treaſure muſt neceſſarily attend our maintaining a continental War, in Conjunction only with a few exhauſted Allies, againſt the united Forces and Intereſt of France and the Houſe of Auſtria!

What, for God's ſake, can it be expected that in theſe Circumſtances we ſhall be able to do, even though the Increaſe of our national Debt, and the Hazard we thereby run of domeſtick Ruin, were Matters of no Conſideration? By ſending a large Fleet into the Baltick we might perhaps over-awe the Swedes and Ruſſians, and thereby prevent their acting forcibly againſt Pruſſia.

3   By

By keeping another large Fleet at Home, and Troops continually ready for Embarkation, or by keeping thofe Troops ftifling on Board Tranfports, and hovering on the *French* Coafts, we might keep them from fending fo formidable a Reinforcement to their Armies in *Germany*, as perhaps they might otherwife do. How little may all this avail! How fhort may it fall of counterballancing the Expence!

The King of *Pruffia* does not want, at prefent, the united Forces of all his Enemies to keep him low enough ; and to crufh him entirely was, perhaps, never the Intent of any. At leaft, fo it has appeared from all the Motions of the *Swedes* and *Ruffians*, and even of the *French* themfelves. Without the Affiftance, therefore, of the *Ruffians* and *Swedes*, the Emprefs-Queen will, in all human Probability, prove a tolerable Match for the *Pruffian* Hero, in his prefent State of Depreffion, Lofs, and Fatigue.

The Advantages, however, which his Caufe is likely to gain, by our taking a Step of that Nature, (fuppofing by the Way too, that it might. give no Umbrage to the Court of *Denmark*) will· evidently never compenfate for the Expence we muft be at on the Occafion ; fince, if the *Auftrian* Troops fhould find the *Pruffian* full Employment, the *Ruffians* would moft probably, as they have hitherto done in like Circumftances, remain voluntarily inactive ; and, if the contrary fhould happen, it might not be in our Power to oblige them to defift from fulfilling their Engagements with their Allies, in a

E   Caufe

Caufe which they feem earneftly to have efpoufed, on Principles not very diftant from thofe of Self-Prefervation and private Intereft.

With refpect alfo to our Expeditions on the *French* Coaft ; the Number of Troops we muft ourfelves employ therein, will as effectually prevent us reinforcing our national Troops in *Germany,* as thofe Expeditions will hinder the Enemy's fending fufficient Reinforcements to theirs : So that, if a continental War muft be carried on, it may differ to us very little, whether we maintain an additional Number of Troops in *Weftphalia,* or harrafs them out with Embarkations and Re-embarkations on fruitlefs Expeditions againft the Coafts of *Brittany* and *Normandy.* Nay, perhaps, it might be even better to do the former, that, in the mean Time, our Fleets may be better employed.

But let us employ our naval Force in the beft Manner we can ; though we ftrip the Enemy of the few Settlements they have left, they have no better Method of avenging themfelves, or of obtaining the Reftitution of any thing at a Peace, but by invading the Dominions of *Great Britain* or *Hanover.*

As to the former ; the prefent Condition of their Fleet feems to have entirely incapacitated them for making the Attempt. Let us not put too much Confidence, however, in our own Advantages, or the Weaknefs of the Enemy. The Race does not always belong to the apparently Swift, or the Battle to the Strong. It is true, the

moft

moſt timid of our Fellow-countrymen, even ſuch as have been under a conſtant Pannic, ever ſince the Beginning of the War, on account of a threatened Invaſion, are now cured of their Fears, and, ſince the Defeat of *Conflans*'s Squadron, begin to triumph in their Security.

It does not yet follow, that what cannot be executed To-day, may not be, neverthelefs, fucceſsfully attempted To-morrow. There is no Man in *England*, indeed, leſs apprehenſive of ſuch an Event than myſelf; although I do not think the Difficulty of it, even in the Circumſtances the *French* Marine now is, ſo great as is generally conceived. But, whatever are the Difficulties, while it is not totally impracticable, who can tell what Opportunity our future Operations may give them? Or what Reaſon we may not have to repent the laſt Efforts of deſpairing Poverty and diſappointed Ambition?

Suppoſing, however, the Hydra of Rebellion unable to lift up its Head; ſuppoſing the deſtructive Monſter of Invaſion, at which we have ſo often trembled, be a mere Chimera, while we keep our Eyes on *Germany*, we ſhall behold ſufficient Cauſe to embrace the firſt, as the beſt, Opportunity of making a Peace.

At all Events, *Hanover* muſt be protected or redeemed, and *Pruſſia* be preſerved from Deſtruction. This muſt be done too by us. None elſe either will, or can do it; and if the Enemy ſhould prove to have the longeſt Sword on the Continent, (the Probability of which, as I have

already

already obferved, is greatly againft us) what is likely to become of our Conquefts at a Peace?

With Fire in your Eyes, and Impatience in your Hearts, methinks I hear fome few of you (diftinguifhed by your, at prefent, unfafhionable Antipathy to continental Connections) cry out on this Reflection, " What are *Pruffia* and *Ha-*
" *nover* to *Great Britain?* What is their Intereft
" to ours, that we fhould renounce the Conquefts
" obtained at our own Expence, and with the
" Lives of our Fellow-countrymen, to procure
" them Indemnification and Security? What is
" the real Protection or Afliftance either of them
" can afford us in Time of War? What do we
" get by them in a Time of Peace? What are
" the reciprocal good Offices they can do us for
" fuch important Services?"

What think you, my Countrymen, of the Proteftant Caufe in *Germany?* Is it not worth your Care and Support? Would you not moft willingly give up one Branch of your Commerce? none of your newly-acquired Settlements? not a Sugar-Ifland, or a Diftrict in *Canada,* to pre-ferve from Ruin, or reward the Magnanimity of that Hero, for whofe Succefs you have publicly put up your Prayers, for whofe Victo-ries you have made fuch extravagant Rejoicings, and for the Support of whofe Caufe you have fo generoufly propofed, and fo liberally promoted, pecuniary Subfcriptions?

If Things are really come to that Pafs in *Ger-many,* that the Ruin of the King of *Pruffia* will be be foon followed by the Ruin of the Proteftant Religion in the Empire, it may not have been without Reafon, perhaps, that you have been told, " That whatever Conquefts we have made, " or may ftill make, upon the *French*, except- " ing only *North America*, fhould be looked " upon as given back to *France*, for a moft im- " portant Confideration, if it can be the Means " of extricating the King of *Pruffia* from any " unforefeen Diftreffes *." But you will be perverfe and fceptical enough, perhaps, to doubt the Truth of the above Suppofition ; you will be curious enough to afk, in what Particular has the Proteftant Caufe appeared fo imminently endan- gered by the Circumftances of the prefent War? Or, if it really has been in any Danger, what are the Steps its pretended Champion has taken, in what has he appeared zealous to fupport it? In what Refpect have the Interefts of the Proteftant Re- ligion been fhewn to be the Motive, Means, or End of the prefent War?

I cannot, indeed, give a fatisfactory Anfwer to thefe Queftions. I fhall wave it therefore, and afk in my Turn, what you think of the Danger in which the Balance of Power muft be, of being entirely overthrown, unlefs fupported on one Side of its Beam by the Force and Riches of *Great Britain?*

Equally impatient as about the Interefts of Religion, you reply, by afking me further, why *Great Britain* is to be always the heavy Weight at the fhort End of the Lever? " What, fay

* Letter to *Two Great Men,* p. 41.

" you,

" you, have we to do with the Jealousies and
" Quarrels of Princes, who, left to themselves,
" would maintain the Balance of Power among
" each other, for their own Sake without us?
" Is it not enough for us to keep up this Ba-
" lance on the Ocean and among the maritime
" Powers? And is it not much too much, to
" take upon us, on every Occasion, to set our-
" selves up to be Arbiters, in the Disputes ari-
" sing between all the Powers of *Europe*?"

These are Questions, my good Friends, that
have been asked a thousand Times, and a Thousand Times answered. Indeed, the most puny
Politician of the present Times will furnish you
with Store of Reasons, as they are called, for our
continental Embarrassments. As none of them,
however, have ever appeared very satisfactory to
me, I cannot flatter myself they will be convinc-
ing to you, I shall not therefore intrude on your
Patience to repeat them.

Thus far, nevertheless, we are obliged to al-
low, that the Protection of *Hanover* might justify
our entering into defensive Alliances with continental Powers, if those Alliances answered the
End, and we could by their Means effectually
obtain the Protection sought; but to pay Subsidies, to maintain a numerous Body of national
Troops in *Westphalia* or *Flanders*, and, after all,
to miss of that Protection, and be obliged to re-
deem that Electorate, by giving up the Conquests
we may have made in other Parts of the World;
this is surely disagreeable enough to think of.

And

And yet fo are we circumftanced, that, however earneftly or reafonably we may wifh, as *Englifhmen*, that no fuch dead Weight, as the Protection of *Hanover* and Support of our infufficient Allies, were link'd to the Profperity of thefe Iflands, it is impoffible, in our prefent Situation, to fhake it off, without breaking all thofe Bonds of Honour, Juftice, and Gratitude, that ought to be revered among Nations. In Favour of the *Hanoverians* it is not unjuftly remarked, that their Country has been attacked, only becaufe it belonged to the King of *Great Britain* ; and that it would be cruel and inhuman to leave them to fuffer from the Confequences of Quarrels originally *Britifh.*

Refpecting the King of *Pruffia* alfo, and our other Allies, even fuppofing our Connections with them only neceffary on the Account of *Hanover*, the fame Plea holds good in their Favour.

Hence it behoves us to bear the Burthen, we yet have fo much Reafon to lament, in the beft Manner we can ; and to make it as light as poffible. *Feras, non culpes, quod vitare non poteft.*

Though the Support of the Proteftant Intereft, or the Balance of Power in *Germany*, therefore, fhould not affect us, let us comfort ourfelves with the Contemplation on thofe ineftimable Bleffings, which have been derived from the Succeffion of the Proteftant Line to the Throne of thefe Kingdoms. Let us confider, that *Hanoverians* and *Englifhmen* have an equal Title to the Protection of the fame gracious Sovereign ; and that, burthenfome as their Connections are to the latter,

we

we might have been much lefs able to bear them, if, in Default of the *Hanover* Succeffion, Popery and arbitrary Power had feated themfelves on the Throne of *Great Britain.* And hence alfo, let us endeavour with Patience, to look upon the Interefts of this Kingdom as, at the prefent Juncture, infeparably connected with that of his Majefty's *German* Dominions and thofe of his Allies.

While I am defirous, however, that we fhould without grumbling fubmit to Neceffity, I am very unwilling that we fhould imagine the Neceffity greater than it really is ; or that becaufe it is expedient for us to do fomething to fupport the Intereft of our Allies, we fhould facrifice every Thing to it, by forgetting our own.

I prefume, that if I have not demonftrated the abfolute Neceffity, I have at leaft fhewn, plainly enough, the Expediency, if it were in our Power, of putting an immediate End to the War ; and the little Probability there is of our being hereafter in a Situation more promifing of an advantageous Peace ; 1 fhall now, therefore, beg your Patience, my Fellow-countrymen, while I communicate thofe Reafons on which my Apprehenfions, of our trifling away the prefent Opportunity, are grounded, and endeavour to point out the Means whereby, I conceive, fo defirable an Event may moft probably be brought about, and that to our leaft Difadvantage.

With refpect to the former ; let me afk, if thofe Apprehenfions are not too juftly founded ? Have we not, in the firft Place, too much Reafon to

fear

fear that, flushed with our late extraordinary Suc-
cesses, we may pertinaciously infist on Conditions,
which the most artful Negotiators will not be able
to procure us ? Or, at least, that whatever Conditions it may be thought proper to stipulate, they
will be proposed, and infisted on, in such a Manner as to raise infurmountable Difficulties, and
protract the Negotiation of the Treaty ?

Have not already our Great Men, as well as
the Public, been addressed by Patriots, real or
pretended, in order to excite a Spirit of national
Pride, by which our Interest may be facrificed to
our Vanity ? Have we not heard some talk in
the unadvised and haughty Strain of demanding
Hostages, before we know in what Particular any
may be neceffary ; and of requiring the Demolition of *Dunkirk* as a Preliminary to Treaty ?

Have we not heard others, equally fanguine and
imperious, advise our infisting on having the Congrefs of the Negotiators held in *London* ; on having the Articles of the Treaty debated in Parliament ; and on fubjecting the Plenipotentiaries to
the Mortification of dancing Attendance on the
Refolutions of an Houfe of Commons ? Surely
nothing of this Kind is the effential and neceffary
Prelude to a good Peace ! I hope no fuch impolitic Pertinacity will reduce us to the Neceffity of
acceding to a bad one !

But what if the *French* were indeed fo humbled
as to fue for Peace in the moft abject Manner ;
what if we could impofe our own Terms in our
own Method ; would it be of any good Confe-

F   quence

quence to this Nation, to behave, on such an Occafion, with Haughtinefs and Infolence ? The Fortifications of Dunkirk have, indeed, long afforded a glaring Inftance of the Enemy's Breach of Faith and the Regard they pay to the moft folemn Treaties. It might not, therefore, be improper to infift on their Demolition as a Preliminary to Treaty, were there any Probability it would be complied with, or were it not likely to delay its Conclufion.

But the Suppofition of the Enemy's fubmitting to fuch a Propofal, were it made, is ridiculous * ; and, were it not fo, the Delay occafioned by putting it in Execution might prove of much greater Confequence to this Nation, than even giving up that Circumftance entirely.

Nature feems herfelf determined, in Spite of the Efforts of the moft able and approved Engineers, to choak up that Port; fo that there is not the leaft Appearance, at prefent, of its being ever made capable of receiving Ships of Force or Burden; and deftroy the Fortifications and Works as you pleafe, it will be always in a State to afford, in a very fhort Time, a fecure neftling Place for fmall Privateers.

Suppofing, neverthelefs, that we do not think it fafe to truft to the dilatory Operations of Nature, all that it can be prudent to do, is to

* It cannot be imagined that any Nation is fo ignorant and fottifh, as not to know that the weakening its Hands before a Negotiation for Peace, is not the Way to fecure it good Terms in that Negotiation. *See Remarks on a Letter to Two Great Men*, p. 15.

make

make the Demolition of this Port an Article in the Treaty; but it never can be fo, to infift on it as a Preliminary. For, let me repeat it again, it is highly expedient for us to haften the Peace by every Method confiftent with our Honour and Intereft: And I fhould be forry to find my Countrymen had fo little Share of Solidity and good Senfe, as to think thefe dependant on Punctilio's of this Nature.

Let us not conceive that, were it in our Power thus to mortify the Enemy, their abject Compliance with our unprofitable Demands would make them hereafter more afraid or afhamed of fhuffling with Treaties, or of breaking their Faith with us, when Opportunity fhould enable them to do it with Impunity. We ought to know the French Nation too well to think fo.

Their Infincerity, and that Art they are Mafters of to extricate themfelves out of Difficulties, which they have fubmitted to by the moft folemn Treaties, is fo notorious, that even Hoftages themfelves might be no fufficient Security for the effectual Performance of any Part of a Treaty, which they might fee their Advantage to break.

So good a Reafon as this for our accepting them, however, is not even affigned for the propofed Demand. No: The Motive is merely vain-glorious and impertinent. At the laft Peace we condefcended to fend Hoftages to Paris as Pledges of our good Faith to bind us in the Performance of an Article, to which the Enemy had

it

it not in their Power to compel us: Now to efface this imaginary Stain on our National Character, we are advised to demand Hostages of them, not as a Security for their performing any Thing we have not in our Power to compel them to do, but merely for the Sake of Parade, and that the good People of London and Westminster may have something to stare at.

If we have really reduced the Enemy so low as to kiss our Footstool, while we sit securely deliberating at Leisure on the Terms of a Peace, let us not shew them, by accepting Hostages on any Account, that we think they dare to trifle with us in the Performance of every Article of the Treaty.

Instead of reflecting on our former Condescension as disgraceful to our National Character, let us regard that Circumstance only as a tacit Confession that the Enemy were in no Condition to enforce Respect to the Treaty by other Means. And if the Vanity of the French will still make them construe it otherwise, let them comfort themselves, and boast to other Nations, with Reflections on their Importance at the last Peace, for the Loss of the more substantial Advantages we may reap by that which is at hand.

I might give another, and perhaps a better, Reason why unnecessary and useless Hostages ought not to be insisted on. Indeed I could wish never to have so insidious and dangerous an Animal as a French Man of Quality reside at our Court, or even in our Country, unless very

closely

clofely confined, on any Occafion or Pretence
whatever.

Need I explain myfelf? What have not the
French learned of our national Weaknefs by re-
fiding among us! How have we not laid ourfelves open to the Enemy by carefling even our
Prifoners of War!

But you defpife the Power, the Genius, the
Arts of thefe reduced, impotent, infignificant
People. You laugh at the diftant Confequences
of my Infinuations. Alas! my Countrymen,
how foon and how greatly is your Note changed!
How little a while is it ago, fince an infignificant French Man, landing at one of our Out-
Ports would have been imagined the Fore-runner
of an Invafion, or his known Departure been
conftrued into the Prelude of a fpeedy Rebellion!

How little a while ago is it fince, dejected by
Ill Succefs, one would have thought, by the
Virulence of your Complaints and the Loudnefs
of your Clamours, that you were on the Brink
of Deftruction!

I do not, I need not, afk what has produced
this extraordinary Change. I admit, in great
Part, the Juftice of your Motives and rejoice in
the Concurrence of fuch a Number of glorious
and fortunate Events. But with all this, let us
remember to what kind of Caufes thefe Events
have been owing. Neither the Perfons or Meafures of the Adminiftration have been *fo much
changed* as to give us any Reafon to depend on
the fuperior Wifdom at the Helm. Or, were

it

it fo, Men ftill are Men, the beft fometimes forget, and the Wifeft of them are not immortal. Let us not, therefore, grown imperious by cafual Succefs, wantonly infult the Enemy, or enhance the Terms of our Demand; left, being obliged hereafter to accept of much lefs, we fhould bring upon ourfelves that Contempt in which we now hold the late idle Gafconades of the Enemy.

Far be it from me to mean to throw out any invidious Infinuations againft refpectable Characters. Far be it from the Reader, alfo, to think me fo little of an Englifhman, as not to rejoice, equally with the moft fanguine of my Countrymen, in our prefent Superiority over the Enemy. It is, indeed, for this very Reafon; it is becaufe I take fo great a Part in the Honour and Intereft of my Country, that I am anxious to prevent, if poffible, any Diminution of its prefent Superiority and Glory.

Tenacious of our prefent Advantages, therefore, let us behave with Refolution; but not Haughtinefs. Elevated by Conqueft, let us preferve our acquired Dignity, by not ftooping fo low as to pique the Vanity of the vaineft Court in the Univerfe, in captioufly ftickling for Trifles: And if any Thing muft be given up to facilitate fo neceffary an Event as a Peace, let our Conceffions be made with as good a Grace as poffible.

Think not, I hold National Honour cheap; or that, leaft of all, I would have victorious
Britons

Britons fubmit to Indignities. The Occafion cannot demand it. We do not fue for, but fhould offer, Terms of Pacification. But I fee fome of you look grave, my Countrymen, at my talking of Conceffions, as a Matter almoft indifpenfible. You are willing, perhaps, to re- ftore *nothing*. I hope you will not be obliged to give up *much*: Nay, were a Treaty of Peace now actually on the Carpet, perhaps, an able Negotiator might find a Neceffity of reftoring but *little*: but I tremble for the Delay. I trem- ble at the Confequences of the War in Germany: At the Clofe of the laft War the Miniftry gave up Cape Breton. The Nation in general, and the People of New-England in particular, were diffatisfied with this Conceffion. But might not the Miniftry, at that Time, have excufed them- felves, in the Manner Demofthenes once did on a fimilar Occafion; might they not have faid, " It is not we that give up Cape Breton; it is " the Neceffities of the Times; it is the fatal " Effects of the Rebellion; it is the Battle of " *Fontenoy*; the Siege of *Bergen-op-Zoom*; it is " the Cowardice and Impotence of the *Dutch*; " it is the Security of *Hanover* that give up " *Cape Breton.*"

God grant that, by any finifter Event, the prefent, or any future, Miniftry may not have as good a Plea, for giving up the more confide- rable Advantages we are now poffeffed of. But let thofe who have the greateft Averfion to Con- tinental Connections (if any can have greater

than

than myfelf) reflect on the Confequence of Hanover's falling again into the Hands of the
French. Let them reflect on the Confequence
of the Dutch being hereafter impolitickly in-
duced to do fomething, which the French will
conftrue into a Breach of Neutrality *. It is
impoffible for us to think of a Peace without
procuring the Reftitution of the Electorate, or
providing for the Security of a daftardly and
impotent Ally. And can we do either without
making the Enemy fome valuable Confideration?

Nay, who can think of a Peace without in-
cluding the Reftitution of Minorca? and will
the French infift on nothing in the Room of it?
Doubtlefs they will: and certainly muft have it too.

But you object that Hanover is not yet in the
Enemy's Hands, that the Dutch have taken no
Part in our Quarrel, and that probably neither
of thefe Circumftances may ever happen. I hope
we fhall be able to fay we fee no Appearance of
either, this Time Twelvemonth.

It matters, however, little whether we are
obliged to give up any of our Conquefts, to ob-

---

* There is perhaps more fear of this, than the Publick
in general imagine. The late grumbling, and half infolent,
Tone of this Republick is changed. In Conjunction with
our Enemy, they imagined they might have controuled our
Authority at Sea. But fince the French Navy has been fo
terribly reduced, their Fears are prevalent; and, acquiefcing
in our Superiority, they feem more ready to oblige us, by
infulting the Enemy, than it is our Intereft they fhould. It
is not long fince they were juft on the Point of unadvifedly
feizing fome Cannon belonging to the French, in its tranf-
port through their Territories.

t in

tain the Reſtitution of Hanover and Security for
any of our Allies; or are neceſſitated to ſpend
the Value of thoſe Conqueſts in their Defence and
Protection. Before we form haſty Reſolutions,
therefore, to give up none of our Acquiſitions
for a preſent Peace, but to keep them at the Hazard of prolonging the War; let it be calmly
deliberated, whether we may not in the End be
Sufferers by ſuch Conduct; and that, inſtead of
our being conſidered hereafter as, in this Inſtance,
juſtly tenacious of the Honour and Intereſt of our
Country, we may not, in lamenting the Conſequences, reflect on ourſelves as acting under the
Influence of pertinacious Inſolence and invincible
Obſtinacy. *Aut minus animi, aut plus potentiæ.*

Again, as to the Place where, or the Perſons
by whom, a Peace is to be negotiated; it matters
leſs that we ſhould make a vain-glorious Choice,
in either of theſe Particulars, than that in both we
ſhould conſult Expedition, and the Expediency
of Terms.

Here alſo a thouſand Difficulties are ſtarted,
that can ſerve only to protract the Negotiation:
The greateſt Difficulty, however, is not to know
what Terms it is our Intereſt to demand, or con-
ſent to; but to prevail on the Enemy to accede
to ſuch Terms, as every Man in *England* knows
we ought to get, if we can.

To effect this, doubtleſs, all the Abilities of
the moſt artful Negociators are requiſite: But I
cannot think ſuch Abilities excluſively annexed
to the Perſon of any particular Miniſter of State,

G   whoſe

whofe Office would prevent his attending a Congrefs at the Hague, or elfewhere.

It is pretended further, that the indefinite and equivocal Manner of Expreffion, common to former Treaties, might be avoided in this, by our taking Time for fufficient Deliberation, and debating the Terms of each Article in Parliament *. I will not deny it. It is poffible that by making the whole Body of the Reprefentatives of the Kingdom, in a Manner, Negotiators, the Articles of the Treaty might be better expreffed, and attended with greater Precifion than otherwife; but the Query ftill recurs, whether the Advantages we are likely to gain thereby will compenfate for the Danger of the Delay fuch a Method of Negotiation muft neceffarily caufe, in bringing the Treaty to a Conclufion?

Will not our Deliberations, in that Cafe, too much refemble thofe of fome Republican States, from the Nature of whofe Conftitution we find them fo long debating about War and Peace, till they often lofe the Opportunity of Vengeance meditated in the one, and the Advantages they propofed to fecure by the other.

I do not deny that Precifion in the Terms and Expreffions of a Treaty are material, and neceffary to be well attended to: But, however indifpenfible it may be in Cafes determinable by eftablifhed Laws and equitable Courts of Juftice, I will venture to fay it is not fo effential in Matters of Agreement between Nations, wherein

* See Reafons why the approaching Treaty of Peace fhould be debated in Parliament.

the

the *Lex ultima regum*, the Sword of Power, determines much oftener than that of Juſtice.

Can we think that the *French*, had they wiſely conſidered they were not a Match for us in *North-America*, would have taken Advantage of the indefinite Terms of the Treaty of *Utrecht*, to make Inroads on *Nova Scotia* and the Territories of *New England* and the *Ohio?*

There is a wide Difference between the Preciſion required in wording the polemical Themes of Academics, or in drawing up a Bill in Parliament, and that acquired in the Terms of Treaties between Sovereigns. And I make no doubt that, by our keeping Poſſeſſion of all *Canada*, by Virtue of an Article, however indefinitely expreſſed in the Treaty, we ſhall be more advantaged, and the Peace will be more laſting, than if we gave back the leaſt Part of it, however limited it might be, even by actual Surveys and Land-Marks erected on the Spot.

For, be the Articles of the Treaty as definite as Words can make them, there is no doubt that the French will make little Scruple of breaking them when their Intereſt and Ambition interfere with the *Letter*, and either is ſeconded by their Power.

Could any Thing be more preciſe and definite than the Article relating to the Demolition of *Dunkirk*, in former Treaties? And yet did they not readily break it, and that in the Face of all *Europe*, without bluſhing?

The Experience of two Centuries paſt may, indeed, ſerve to convince us (if we yet need any

farther

farther Retrospect to be convinced of it) that nothing but Power and Resolution on our Part, to compel them to be just, can keep them so.

Our principal Business, therefore, is to obtain a Peace on Terms that will in some Measure keep themselves; that is, enable us to make the Enemy, at all Times, respect our own Construction of them.

Now the present Circumstances are so favourable to us in this Particular, that we ought to trust nothing needlesly to the future, in hopes of better; lest, like the Dog in the Fable, anxious, with our Mouths already full, after more, we are obliged to relinquish what we have already acquired. *Ne umbra pro corpore.*

I shall next, therefore, my Countrymen, endeavour to point out the Means, whereby an Event so desireable, so requisite to the Welfare of this Nation, may possibly be brought about.

I flatter myself you are already convinced of the little Probability there is that the French will accept of a Peace, and sit down with their present Losses. The Outlines of the Prospect of the Consequences of the German War, which I have not unjustly drawn in their Favour, are yet greatly so. Minorca too is in their Hands. Something must, therefore, necessarily be given up to prevail on them to enter immediately into Terms of Accommodation.

What this is to be, becomes thus the principal Object of our present Consideration. Much has already been said and written on this Subject.

The

The Importance of our several Acquisitions have been debated, and that of each been enhanced and undervalued, in turn. This Confideration, however, is not the only one we should attend to, in the present Cafe. In order to bring the Enemy to a speedy Accommodation, it is necessary to confider as well the real as imaginary Value of those Acquifitions to them.

That which is of the least Importance to us is doubtless what we should the soonest chuse to relinquish : But if this, at the same Time, be equally unimportant to the Enemy, they will no doubt set as just a Value on the Conceffion as we.

It has been maintained, by some of our Patriots, that no Part of our Conquests on the Continent of North America, should be given up on any Confideration whatever ; while the Infignificancy of *Senegal* and *Goree*, and the inferior Confequence of *Guadeloupe* have been offered, as Reafons for our relinquishing those Places.

On the other Hand, again, it has, with no less Appearance of Reafon, been alledged that the single Ifle of *Guadeloupe* is of more Importance to this Nation than all *Canada*. It is said that the whole Trade of Canada confifts in that of Furs and Skins, and fell short in its most flourishing State of 140,000 l. a Year ; while *Guadeloupe* produces more Sugar than any of our Iflands, except *Jamaica* ; by which Branch of Trade alone 300,000 l. *per Annum* might be cleared by our Merchants : For that, having fufficient from

our

our own Iflands to fupply our Home Confumption, the whole Sugar Produce of Guadeloupe
might be exported, and would confequently be
fo much clear Money to Great Britain *.

Might we not afk, however, on this Occafion,
at what Rate is our Home Confumption at prefent fupplied? Were Sugars cheaper, there is
little Reafon to doubt our Home Confumption
would be much more confiderable.

Has it not, alfo, been long notorious that our
own Iflands would produce much more Sugar
than they have lately done, had not injurious
Combinations been entered into, to prevent the
bringing fuch Quantities to Market as muft
lower the Price?

I have been further very credibly informed
that, notwithftanding it is pretended by many
that the Lands of *Guadeloupe* are much better
than thofe of our own Sugar Iflands, yet its Sugars are confiderably lefs valuable than ours, or
thofe of the Ifland of *Martinico*.

I will not pretend, however, to affert the fuperior Value and Importance of Canada, taken
folely in a commercial Point of View: Since in
Guadeloupe they raife, befides Sugar, great
Quantities of Indigo, Cotton, Coffee, Ginger,
&c. all which is not only fent to the European
Markets; but a confiderable Trade is alfo carried on between that Ifland and the Caraccas, and
other Parts of the Spanifh Main, which Trade
is wholly confined to the Manufactures of Europe, the Returns for which are chiefly in Ready

---

* See Remarks on a Letter to Two Great Men, p. 40.

Money,

Money. If to this we add that the Slaves now in the Ifland are alone, at the lowest Valuation, worth upwards of One Million Sterling, there is no doubt but Guadeloupe is of more Confequence in a commercial View than Canada.

As an Acquifition, alfo, that may be of Service in a Time of War, *Guadeloupe* is by no Means inconfiderable. The infinite Difadvantage it has been of to us during the prefent, is univerfally allowed. The Ifland of *La Defirade*, being the firft Land ufually made by our Ships bound to the Weft-Indies, they are eafily perceived in their Courfe from thence, by the Privateers of Guadeloupe ; which could not have a more convenient Station to annoy us, in this particular, than that Ifland.

Notwithftanding thefe Confiderations, however, I muft give my Voice entirely for thofe who would rather give up Guadeloupe, with every other Acquifition we have made, or may make, in the Weft-Indies, than part with one fingle foot of Canada.

In my Reafons for it I differ, however, from thofe who affect to efteem it important, on account either of its Trade, the Number of Inhabitants, or the Fertility of its Soil ; the principal Objection that appears to me, againft giving up any Part of Canada is the Danger we thereby run of giving Occafion, in a few Years, for another War: An Objection that does not equally oppofe the relinquifhing *Guadeloupe*. It has been faid that, by eftablifhing proper Limits,

and

and fecuring them properly, we might very prudently reftore *Canada* to the French. But the
Misfortune is, that no Limits we can make in
that Part of the World would be proper, for the
very Reafon, that it is impoffible they can at prefent be properly fecured, without putting both
Nations to an Expence much greater than the
prefent Value of the Matter in difpute.

It is alfo much to be doubted whether, if this
were practicable, the French would not be as
willing to defift entirely from the Demand as to
be effectually reftrained within thofe Bounds to
which it is abfolutely neceffary for us to con-
fine them.

If they fhould give up their long-fince-projec-
ted Scheme of elbowing our Colonies, and of
edging down by Degrees to the Sea-Coaft, Canada will certainly be of little Advantage.

But, fuppofing the two Courts could come to a
right Underftanding in this Point, and be fatif-
fied with the Limits affigned; we have an Exam-
ple, in the Manner in which the prefent War com-
menced, how very foon it is likely to be difturbed.

It is well known what Kind of Men our Colo-
nifts, and in particular the Traders with the In-
dians, generally are; nor do we fuppofe thofe
belonging to the French are a Jot more fcrupu-
lous in their Morals. Now, let the Harmony
fubfifting between the two Courts be ever fo well
eftablifhed, or kept up in Europe; let them be
ever fo defirous of remaining on good Terms
with each other; how long can we promife ourfelves

felves this Harmony will continue; when, on the firſt Temptation of any conſiderable Profit, the adventuring Borderers will inſult each other? their Complaints will be heard by their reſpective Sovereigns, and the two Nations be involved again in a ruinous and bloody War.

Hence, although, by reſtoring Guadeloupe, we ſhould in Fact give up an Acquiſition of more Importance, in almoſt every other Conſideration; yet the Expediency of our taking ſuch Meaſures as will not only procure an advantageous, but ſecure a laſting, Peace, requires that Guadeloupe, with the other Iſlands attendant on that Conqueſt, be rather reſtored entire to the Enemy, than that we ſhould give up one Foot of *Canada.*

As it is of great Moment, however, toward the Negotiation of the Treaty, that we ſhould conſider in what light the French look on theſe two different Conceſſions; perhaps it will be found that, ſeeing the little Proſpect there is of their ever ſucceeding in their grand Scheme, againſt our too powerful Colonies in North-America, they will give up the Deſign; and, conſidering the vaſt Importance Guadeloupe is of to their Commerce, they will more readily enter into this Meaſure than the other.

As they will require, alſo, the Convenience which *Senegal* and *Goree* afforded them, of procuring Slaves for their Weſt-India Iſlands, the Reſtoration of thoſe Places, added to that of *Guadeloupe,* &c. will appear ſo valuable a Conſideration, that we have all the Reaſon in the

World

World to think they will, on such an Offer, enter gladly into Terms of Pacification, and sit down contented with the Loss of their Ships preceding the Declaration of War.

On giving up, further, Cape Breton, after demolishing the Fortifications, and on renewing their Privilege of Fishing, &c. on the Banks and Coast of Newfoundland, they will also very probably resign *Minorca* in exchange, and be so ready to concur in the necessary Measures to a speedy Accommodation, that the Empress Queen will think it prudent, also, to enter into the like with the King of *Prussia*.

As the latter may, even at present, stand in need of our Assistance, it will doubtless be requisite to lend a helping Hand to this brave Ally; which, rather than give any further Advantage to the *French*, should be done by Means of a Sum of Money, to be paid to the Court of *Vienna*, and another to the Elector of *Saxony*.

I prefer this Method to any other, as ready Money will be so likely to be accepted of ; and the Sums we need give will not probably amount to a twentieth Part of what it may cost us to carry on the War, if no such Steps are taken.

I doubt not but many of you will break out on this Proposal, and exclaim against it, as an Indignity. What! after all our Success and Conquests, you will say, shall we at last shamefully *buy* a Peace?

But let me advise you, my good Friends, to recollect that celebrated Adage, so familiar in

every

every economical Nation, ' A Penny faved is a
' Penny got :' And reflect that a good Peace,
cheaply bought, will redound more to the Honour and Advantage of this Kingdom, than all
the Bargains we may make in the Continuation
of the War, by the inhuman Purchafe of Rapine
and Blood.

In the prefent Succefs of our Arms, the Dif-
burfement of Money cannot be fuppofed a re-
proachful Circumftance ; fince it will appear as
well a Proof of your fuperior Wealth, as be
evident to all *Europe*, that the Purchafe of a
Peace is not neceffary for own Sake, but only
for our Allies.

The *Quota*, deftined to the Indemnification of
the Elector of Saxony, muft alfo be efteemed
rather as a Mark of Generofity than Meannefs;
and it will doubtlefs appear, in the Eyes of all
the World, as a noble Inftance of ours to relieve
that unfortunate, though perhaps blameable,
Prince. As to the Terms on which the King
of Pruffia and the Emprefs Queen may agree,
with regard to Silefia, I do not fee that we have
any Bufinefs to intermeddle with Particulars.
The former, it has been juftly obferved, has not
been reduced to his prefent Diftrefs in Confequence of his Connections with us ; and, as we
have already been an ufeful Ally, fo, in our
endeavouring thus, at our own Expence, to
bring about a general Pacification, although we
fhould not be able to procure him all he could
wifh, he ought to be content.

Again,

Again, as to the Manner in which *France* and the Court of *Vienna* may agree about sharing the Expences of the War, and their mutual Indemnification; I do not see also that it much concerns us. The French did not move to the Assistance of the Empress Queen, till they had first taken a few Towns in Flanders into their Possession, apparently by Way of Security for the Repayment of their Expences. As their principal Operations, also, have tended rather to distress the Elector of *Hanover*, by Way of avenging their own Cause of Quarrel with *England*, the Empress has doubtless Reason to expect her Towns again at the Peace. But should it prove otherwise, we are too little interested in it to make any farther Concessions, as some inconsistent Politicians would have us, in order to take them out of the Hands of France, and put them into hers.

A British Administration, it has been said *, must tremble at seeing Newport and Ostend become French Property. I would not have it so: And yet it is not every Administration that would tremble at it.

We have had e'er now very great Men at the Helm, who knew little of the real Value or Importance of the Places they have bought, sold, or bartered for, with Foreign Powers. The great Earl of *Clarendon* has assured us, that when *Dunkirk* was sold to the French, it was a good

* Letter to Two Great Men. p. 42.

Par-

Bargain on our Side; and yet, by his own Con-
feſſion, this ſame eminent Stateſman did not
even know whereabouts the Iſle of *Sheepey*, at
the Mouth of the Thames, was ſituated.

I make no ſcruple, however, that our preſent
Adminiſtration are well apprized of the Importance of *Newport* and *Oſtend*, and that they are
under no very great Apprehenſions of there being a Port opened on that Coaſt, from which
this Nation has ſo much hereafter to fear, as to
make it now worth while to ſacrifice any Thing
of Conſequence to prevent its falling into the
Hands of the *French*.

If the Queen of Hungary were, indeed, our
Ally, and had ſuffered in our Cauſe, ſomething
might be ſaid for it: But, as it is otherwiſe, and
we can place no Dependance on her Honour or
Gratitude, who knows but, after we ſhould have
purchaſed the Evacuation of theſe Towns of
 French, ſhe might put them again into their
   Is ſhe not capable of it? *Ingratum ſi*
      mnia dixeris.

   uppoſing it be not quite ſo prudent to
     Flemiſh Towns, now in the Poſſeſſion
       ench, in their Hands, at a Peace; all
 that we can at preſent propoſe to do, is either
on Conſideration of their evacuating them, to
recede from the Demolition of the Fortifications
of Louiſbourg; or in Lieu of it to pay them a
Sum of Money, as a better and more acceptable
Equivalent.

Thus

Thus have I taken a curfory Examination of thofe Circumftances that fhould induce us to haften a Peace, and the Terms which I conceive the Enemy may, at prefent, be brought to accede to. If my Remarks are juft; if my Propofals are reafonable; they will, I doubt not, have their due Weight with the Publick. If they are not fo, it is Pity they fhould. I fhall lefs regret my Lofs of Time and Trouble than the being, in any Degree, inftrumental in mifleading my Fellow-Countrymen, either to their Publick or Private Difadvantage.

I am,

My Friends and Countrymen,

Yours, &c. &c.